Beast Quest®

RonaK
THE TOXIC TERROR

BY ADAM BLADE

ORCHARD

WELCOME TO

Beast Quest

Collect the special coins in this book.
You will earn one gold coin for
every chapter you read.

Once you have finished all the chapters,
find out what to do with your gold coins at
the bac...

With special thanks to Conrad Mason

To Enzo Theroux, a big fan!

www.beastquest.co.uk

ORCHARD BOOKS
Carmelite House
50 Victoria Embankment
London EC4Y 0DZ

A Paperback Original
First published in Great Britain in 2015

Beast Quest is a registered trademark of Beast Quest Limited
Series created by Beast Quest Limited, London

Text © Beast Quest Limited 2015
Inside illustrations by Pulsar Estudio
(Beehive Illustration) © Beast Quest Limited 2015.
Cover illustration by Steve Sims © Beast Quest Limited 2015

A CIP catalogue record for this book is available from
the British Library.

ISBN 978 1 40833 996 1

1 3 5 7 9 10 8 6 4 2

Printed in Great Britain

MIX
Paper from
responsible sources
FSC® C104740

The paper and board used in this book are made from wood
from responsible sources.

Orchard Books
An imprint of Hachette Children's Group
Part of The Watts Publishing Group Limited
An Hachette UK company

www.hachette.co.uk

GWILDOR

GWILDORIAN OCEAN

ON

AND

FISHING
VILLAGE

CONTENTS

Greetings, followers of the Quest,

I am Irina, the Good Witch of Avantia's twin kingdom, Gwildor. This was supposed to be a time of happiness, as we welcomed young heroes Tom and Elenna to our capital city Jengtor. Freya, Tom's mother and Mistress of the Beasts, beamed with pride at the thought of her son's arrival.

She smiles no longer.

Someone else has been awaiting Tom's arrival. We should have known our enemies would choose this moment to strike. Now Freya lies in my chamber, unable to command her Beasts. And Jengtor is under siege from a deadly menace that attacks from the skies.

Our only hope lies with Tom and Elenna, but they are walking right into a trap.

Irina, loyal Witch of Gwildor

THE BROKEN VIAL

Tom clung on tight to Angel's reins as they thundered along the rocky path. The horse was panting, but there was no time to stop and rest. If they delayed now, they would be putting all of Gwildor in mortal danger.

The path dipped and rose again through long swaying grasses on

either side. Tom threw a quick
glance over his shoulder to check
that Elenna was with him. His
friend was crouched low over
her own horse, Star. Her hair
was streaming in the breeze,
and her features were set with
determination. Every now and again,
her eyes flicked up towards the sky.

Tom knew exactly what she was looking for. At any minute, Sanpao's flying pirate ship might come swooping down from the sky and put a stop to their Quest. Tom followed his friend's gaze, and his heart lurched as he saw a dark shape flitting high above.

Phew! It was only a seagull.

Sanpao's probably too busy laying siege to Jengtor, making its innocent citizens suffer for the sake of his own greed...

Tom turned his attention back to the path ahead. *We have to get to Jengtor – and fast.* He couldn't stop thinking of his mother, trapped there in the capital of Gwildor, her body racked with poison from the evil magic of Kensa.

The rocky path veered off to the right, but Tom and Elenna kept heading straight inland. The sun sank lower in the sky, and when they reached the top of a hill, Elenna reined in her horse and let out a gasp. Below, farmland stretched out to the horizon. But the dazzling golden crops of Gwildor were faded and wilted to muddy browns and greens.

"What happened here?" muttered Elenna.

"I don't know," said Tom. "But I have a feeling I know who's responsible..."

Elenna nodded grimly. "Kensa," she said.

"Don't worry," Tom told her. "We won't let her get away with it."

They rode down the hillside. Up close, Tom saw that the crops had all wasted away. In some places they had rotted into a murky slime that smelled so bad that Tom and Elenna

had to cover their noses with their
sleeves.

Angel let out a whinny and slowed
to a canter. The next moment Star
reared up, almost throwing Elenna
from his back. "Whoa there!" she
cried.

*Even the horses can tell that
something's wrong.*

"We'd better stop," said Elenna,
stroking Star's neck to calm him.
"We won't reach Jengtor before
dusk, and the horses need a rest."

Tom glanced up at the sun, which
was turning orange and sinking
closer to the horizon. He knew
his friend was right. He scanned
around and spotted a shallow

watering hole in the next field.

"Look!" he said, pointing. "We can camp there for the night, then set off at sunrise."

Tom's stomach squirmed as they approached the pool. The foul stench in the air got worse the closer they came.

"Poor creature," murmured Elenna, and Tom turned to see a cow lying dead on its side, its eyes shut and its belly swollen. There were others corpses further off.

Tom wished he could heal the animals with the power of the green jewel, but it was obvious that there was nothing he could do for them, even with magic.

Elenna shivered. "Something terrible happened here," she said quietly. "Maybe we shouldn't stay after all."

Tom brought Angel to a halt and dismounted. He crossed to the shallow pool of water and saw that it was thick, murky and green. There was no way they could drink it.

As he stepped back something crunched beneath his foot. Tom bent down and found shattered fragments of glass trodden into the mud.

A broken vial...

At once the sick feeling in his stomach grew ten times worse. The pieces of the vial looked very

familiar indeed. He turned to
Elenna, holding up the fragments
for her to see.

Elenna went pale. "It looks just
like the one with that horrible
magic potion inside, that Kensa
used to conjure up Styro," she said.

"I'm afraid so," said Tom. "And if the potion could turn an ordinary lobster into a deadly lobster Beast..."

"What kind of Beast has Kensa created this time?" Elenna finished for him.

The air seemed to have turned suddenly chilly.

"We'll have to investigate," said Tom. "With my mother sick, there are no Good Beasts to protect Gwildor, so it's up to us to..." He trailed off as he saw something. A short distance away, there were hoofprints in the mud.

Giant hoofprints, far bigger than any horse's, and cloven like a goat's.

Elenna gasped, and looked at him. Tom knew she was thinking the same thing as he was. *Could those belong to the Beast?*

Tom climbed onto Angel's back and they set out in silence, following the tracks away from the watering hole.

"Have you noticed?" said Elenna, as they trotted across the muddy field. "The crops that are closest to the hoofprints are the most rotten."

Tom nodded thoughtfully. "It's almost as though the Beast itself is toxic. Maybe that's causing the decay... But what kind of monster could—?"

"Wait!" Elenna pulled back on the

reins, then pressed a finger against her lips.

Tom strained his ears. Then he heard it too – the clatter of metal against metal.

"It's a sword fight!" he said.

He squeezed his knees into Angel's flanks, and the horse took off, kicking up mud as it sped across the field. Star's hooves pounded the ground close behind. Whatever was going on, Tom hoped they would get there before blood was spilt.

The horses raced up the low brow of a hill. As they crested the rise, Tom saw a crowd of people in the field below, jostling and shouting. There was a clear space in the centre, where two figures were fighting savagely. Tom reined in his horse.

"What in all of Gwildor...?" panted Elenna, as she caught up with him.

"I'm going to try to get closer," Tom told her. He leapt off Angel's back and rushed down the hillside.

"Wait for me!" came Elenna's voice from behind, but Tom kept running. He could see the figures more clearly now. One was an old man, big and strong as an ox. The other was young, fast and wiry. The old man swung a hefty axe with slow, powerful strokes, whilst the younger man danced out of reach, a sword flashing in his hand. Both of them were sweating and panting.

"Come on, Karl!" Tom heard someone shout.

"Get him, Uther!" called another.

Tom reached the crowd and tried to force his way through. "Stop it!" he shouted. "Why are you fighting each other?"

"Stay out of this," growled a big man in a blacksmith's apron. He grabbed Tom with a hairy fist and pushed him backwards.

Tom staggered, then peered between the heads of the crowd. He saw the old man take a mighty swing which buried his axe in the ground. The young man seized his chance, kicking his opponent in the chest

and sending the old man sprawling
back into the mud. Then he leapt
forward, sword raised high, glinting
in the last light of the sun.

ROUGH JUSTICE

Tom whipped out his own sword and drew on the power of the golden boots, feeling the magic surge into his legs. Then he leapt over the crowd, landing in the centre of the circle in a crouch. He swung his sword, just as the victorious fighter's blade came slicing down.

Clang!

The blades met with a shock
that juddered through Tom's arms
and sent the young man stumbling
backwards.

"Stop the fight!" yelled Tom.
The crowd fell silent, and both

fighters stared at him.

"This doesn't concern you," snarled
the young man.

"Leave, stranger!" shouted
someone from the crowd. Murmurs
of agreement sounded all around.

Tom swallowed hard, trying
to stay calm. Up close, he could
see that the young man wore no
armour – just a sheep's-hide tunic
and tough old boots. He was even
younger than Tom had thought,
with wild, windswept hair and a
deep tan, as though he spent all day
outside. The sword he held was old
and battered, with patches of rust
on the blade.

He's no warrior, Tom realised.
More like a farmer, or a shepherd.

He turned to the old man lying on
the ground, who was watching Tom
just as warily as the others. The man
had long silver hair and a beard,
and gentle blue eyes. His axe still

stood buried in the mud, and Tom saw that it was a woodcutter's tool, not a battle-axe.

"You should go," said the old man. He scrambled to his feet and nodded at his opponent. "This is between me and him."

"Kill the boy!" yelled someone, pointing at Tom. "He's standing in the way of justice!"

There was a chorus of metallic scrapes, and Tom saw that several of the men had drawn daggers.

"Please," he said. "I'm just trying to—"

Whoooosh!

An arrow whined above their heads, causing half the crowd to duck.

"No one touch him!" shouted
Elenna.

Tom turned to see his friend had
dismounted and was standing on
the slopes above the circle, glaring

fiercely, another arrow already nocked on her bowstring. "Put the knives away," she demanded. "Unless you want to be pincushions!"

Reluctantly, the men slid the blades back in their sheaths.

"As I was saying," said Tom, "I'm sure no one needs to get hurt. Why are you fighting?"

"It's his fault," spat the young man.

"Liar," growled his opponent.

"One at a time!" said Tom. He pointed to the silver-haired fighter.

"Very well," said the old man. "My name is Uther, champion of the village of Guran. Karl here and his fellow crooks from Hintor have been poisoning our crops."

"The old fool doesn't know what he's talking about," Karl retorted. "If their crops are dying, it's because Guran folk are poor farmers. Always have been!"

Angry muttering broke out among Uther's half of the circle.

"We don't care about their crops," Karl went on. "All I care about is my prize ram. A bunch of Guran rustlers stole it two days ago." He turned on Uther. "You lot have always been jealous of us, because you know Hintor is the best village in all of Gwildor and Guran is nothing but a filthy pigsty!"

"I don't understand," said Tom

quickly, before the argument could get any worse. "Why fight a duel over it? Why not just send for the local judge?"

"We have," said Uther. "But he lives in Jengtor, miles from here. We had no reply."

Tom shot a glance at Elenna. *No wonder there was no reply – the capital is under siege by Sanpao!* He wasn't about to tell Karl and Uther that, though. The last thing they needed was for the villagers to start panicking.

"Hey!" shouted a young voice. It was a little boy with long blond hair, and he was pointing at Tom, his eyes wide. "I know you! You look just like our Mistress of the Beasts. You must be her son, Tom!"

"The famous Tom, is it?" exclaimed Karl, though he didn't

sound impressed. "What are you
doing in Gwildor?

"Is there a Beast on the loose?"
asked Uther.

The crowd stirred, casting nervous glances all around.

"Please don't worry," said Elenna, quickly. "We're just passing through on our way to—"

"I saw it!" shrieked an old woman, from the back of the crowd. "I saw the Beast! Two days ago, out in the fields at dusk, and no one believed me. Not even my own daughter!"

"There's only one Beast that lives near here," said Uther. "And that's Hawkite."

"The Arrow of the Air, they call her," Karl added.

Uther nodded. "It must be that mangy bird that's causing mischief, damaging our crops. Ten to one it was her that took your ram, too!"

"You've got it wrong," said Tom, desperately. "Hawkite's a Good Beast. But do we think there's a new Beast out there."

"A new Beast?" jeered Karl. "Beasts don't grow on trees! You should know that, if you really are a Master of the Beasts. If you won't help us, we'll slay Hawkite ourselves."

"Let's work together," said Uther. "Men of Guran, side by side with the men of Hintor. We'll soon catch this flying menace!" Cheers rang out from both sides of the crowd as Uther held out his hand, and Karl shook it firmly.

"Please, listen to Tom!" Elenna
called out, but the villagers were
already drawing weapons and

chattering excitedly.

"We'll split up," shouted Karl.
"First person to find the Beast, make
as much noise as you can. The rest of
us will come running."

As the villagers strode off into the
gathering darkness, Elenna hurried
to Tom's side. "What now?" she
asked.

"Now we have to find Hawkite,"
Tom told her. "And hope we get to
her before the villagers."

*Because if that Beast turns on
them, they're as good as dead...*

ARROW OF THE AIR

Tom closed his eyes in the dusk and drew on the power of the red jewel in his shield. He reached out with his mind, searching for the Beast.

Where are you, Hawkite?

A distant voice sounded in his head, echoing softly.

Here, Tom. So weak. Help me...

Hawkite's voice was no more than a whisper, and the next moment it was gone entirely.

"Did you find her?" asked Elenna, as Tom blinked and opened his eyes.

"No," said Tom, frowning. "It sounds like the villagers haven't reached her yet, but something's wrong. Wherever she is, she's in trouble."

"So what next?"

Tom thought hard. *There is one clue.* If only there was someone they could ask...

He looked around and saw that a few of the villagers had stayed behind to build a fire. Among them was the blond boy who had recognised Tom. He was gazing shyly at them, as though he wanted to approach but didn't dare.

"Hello there," said Tom, smiling at the boy. "What's your name?"

"Kevan," said the boy. He took a few cautious steps towards them.

"Will you help us find Hawkite, Kevan?" said Elenna. "I'm sure you know this countryside much better than us!"

Kevan blushed but nodded furiously. "I'll help! If Tom says Hawkite's safe, I trust him. I've heard so many stories about you both. I can't believe I'm really here with Tom and Elenna!"

Tom and Elenna shared a glance,

and Tom saw that his friend was doing her best not to laugh.

"Kevan," said Tom, seriously. "Do you know of any caves near here?"

The boy creased his brow in concentration. "Maybe," he said. "Old Gideon the shepherd told me there were some to the west, in a copse of oak trees. I'm not normally allowed out of Hintor."

"Thank you!" said Tom. Kevan grinned and hurried back to his fellow villagers. Tom noticed one or two of them casting suspicious glances at him and Elenna.

"I don't understand," said Elenna, as they mounted their horses. "Why are we looking for caves?"

"Just a hunch," Tom replied. "Hawkite's voice was echoing, as though she were in a big empty space. I think maybe she was hurt and crawled into a cave for safety."

"Good thinking," said Elenna.

They set off, leaving the villagers behind them and galloping west. The stars were coming out in the darkening sky, and before long there was only moonlight to guide them.

Tom shivered as they rode. *If Hawkite really is stuck in a cave, she'll be easy prey for the villagers...*

At last a rocky outcrop rose out of the grasses ahead, surrounded by huge weather-ravaged oak trees. Tom could sense the power of the red jewel throbbing in his shield. *We must be close.*

They pulled up their horses, and Elenna drew in a sharp breath.

"What's that white stuff over there?" she said, pointing.

Tom climbed down and knelt. Scraps of wool clung to the jagged rocks that formed the mouth of a cave.

"It looks like pieces of a ram's fleece," he said, grimly.

"You don't think Hawkite really did kill Uther's ram, do you?" wondered Elenna.

Tom shook his head. "That's impossible. Hawkite's a Good Beast. I think someone must have put the wool here to make it look like it was her fault."

"Something tells me this is Kensa's work," Elenna muttered.

"There's only one way to find out," said Tom, drawing his sword.

Side by side, they crept into the darkness. The air was stale, and Tom almost had to cover his nose at the stench. *Can that be the smell of Hawkite?* If so, something really was wrong with her.

The narrow entrance opened up into a cavernous space beyond, where a shaft of moonlight shone through a chink in the rock, falling on the feathers of the Beast. She lay slumped on the floor, her golden eyes dim and hooded, as though she could barely keep them open.

Through the red jewel, Tom heard Hawkite's dry, dusty croak.

You came. Thank you.

Elenna knelt at the Beast's side, pulled a water canister from her belt and tipped some gently into Hawkite's open beak. "I've never seen her so sick before," she murmured.

"It must be because of my mother," said Tom. A lump formed in his throat. "She's been poisoned, and so all the Good Beasts are suffering too. Their energy is connected to hers."

"Wait – what's that?" said Elenna, whirling around.

Voices! Somewhere outside the cave.

"They've found us," Tom whispered. "That's the last thing we need…"

"Come out!" someone shouted from outside the cave.

Elenna shrugged. "I don't think we have much choice."

They crept out through the tunnel to find a ring of villagers gathered outside, surrounding the cave mouth. Their weapons shone in the moonlight. At the centre was Karl, his rusty blade drawn and pointed straight at Tom.

"Stand aside, Avantians," Karl demanded. "Don't make us hurt you."

Tom and Elenna looked at each other, then shook their heads at the same time.

"No way," said Elenna.

"Hawkite is innocent," Tom told them. "You must let her go."

Karl scowled and pointed at the rocks around the cave. "If she's innocent then how did those scraps of fleece get there? She's murdered my ram!" He nodded to the others, and several of the biggest villagers stepped forward, hefting axes, pitchforks and scythes.

Elenna whipped an arrow from her quiver, and Tom's grip tightened on his sword hilt. Quickly he drew on the power of the red jewel, reaching out to Hawkite with his mind.

Get out of the cave!

But Hawkite made no reply.

"Looks like it's up to us to defend her," said Elenna, grimly.

Tom's heart sank. He didn't want to fight the villagers, but what choice did they have?

Suddenly there was a sound like rolling thunder from behind, and Tom felt the ground shake. A gust of wind came rushing from the cave mouth, sending Tom and Elenna staggering.

"It's an earthquake!" yelled one of the villagers.

Tom grinned. *It's not an earthquake... It's Hawkite!*

He and Elenna threw themselves to the ground as the Beast came flapping out into the open. Her wings beat the air, trying to find a rhythm, as she let out a cry of defiance that forced several of the villagers to cover their ears.

She might be sick, thought Tom, *but she doesn't look it!*

Hawkite took off, shedding a few tail feathers but moving strongly, rising fast and disappearing into

the inky black sky.

"Look out, Tom!" cried Elenna.

Tom rolled over and saw villagers
approaching on all sides, weapons

raised. He scrambled to his feet.

"Traitors!" Karl roared. "You helped the Beast get away!"

Tom snatched up his sword, but before he could swing it pain exploded through his head. He sank to his knees, as a man wielding a club stepped in front of him.

Darkness clouded Tom's vision. Then it swallowed him completely.

4

RAT FOOD

When Tom woke, his head hurt
so much he could barely think.
His breath was hot against some
material that covered his face – a
hood, made from sackcloth.

How long was I unconscious for?
And where am I?

He opened his eyes and found
only more darkness. He flexed

his muscles, trying to move, but something was wrong. Ropes bound his hands and feet. He was upright and spreadeagled.

This isn't good.

"Elenna?" he called out. "Are you there?"

"Tom!" his friend croaked. She was somewhere to his side, and her voice sounded muffled, as though she was hooded too. "They tied us up. Where are we?"

"You'll soon see," growled a new voice.

All of a sudden the hood was ripped from Tom's head. He blinked, adjusting to the flickering light. A circle of faces glared at him, lit by torches that threw ghoulish shadows.

They were in a cavernous wooden building with stacks of hay at one end. *A barn.* The big double doors stood open, and through them Tom could see a sliver of star-studded sky. Turning his head, he saw that he was bound to a heavy wooden cartwheel that leant against the wall. Elenna was trussed up to a second wheel beside him. Their weapons were nowhere to be seen.

"So, Master of the Beasts," sneered Karl. Uther stood with him, and they both looked furious. "Welcome to Hintor! Let's see you magic your way out of this one."

"Let us go!" shouted Elenna. "You've no right to tie us up like this."

"And you had no right to free the Beast that was tormenting us," Uther retorted. "You've left us no choice. We have sent a messenger to

Jengtor. Either Freya comes to slay our Beast in return for your safety, or — "

"Or the pair of you are going to be rat food," Karl interrupted. He smirked. "There are plenty of rodents in this barn, and they'll

be only too happy to sink their teeth into a couple of soft young Avantians like you."

His cronies chuckled.

"I already told you, Hawkite's not to blame," Tom explained. "There must be some other Beast out there. If you just let us go, we can protect you."

"Tom's right!" piped up a voice from the back of the crowd. Kevan pushed his way through, and Tom saw that the little boy's cheeks were stained with tears. "I'm so sorry," he mumbled.

"You need to toughen up, lad," Uther told him. "These adventurers have put Guran and Hintor in terrible danger."

"Come on," said Karl. "Let's leave the Avantians to get some rest. They'll need it if they're to fight off the rats all night."

"Wait!" said Tom, but it was no good. Karl and Uther led the villagers from the barn, dragging Kevan with them.

The blacksmith was last to leave. He slammed the double doors shut, leaving them in darkness. There was a clunking sound as they were locked, and the scraping of a heavy bar being set in place on the other side.

"What now?" Elenna sighed.

Tom only wished he knew. He

strained his muscles, trying to snap the ropes that bound his wrists and ankles, but the bonds were far too thick and tightly tied. He sagged back again. *They've already seen the magic of the Golden Armour,* Tom remembered. *They must have guessed I'd try to use it to escape.*

"We can't give up!" said Elenna. "Jengtor is still under siege. And if Kensa and Sanpao break through Irina's force field, the whole capital will be at their mercy."

"We should have told the villagers," said Tom, glumly. "If they only understood how serious this is..."

"Wait," hissed Elenna. "Look over there!"

Tom strained his eyes, and saw dark shapes scurrying across the

floor. They clustered around the cartwheels, their fur black and greasy, their tails coiling like worms. *Rats!* He felt a shudder run down his spine.

The creatures crept closer, noses twitching, eyes shining hungrily in the darkness. Elenna tried to kick the nearest one away, but the ropes held her tight. Her cartwheel creaked, shifting under her weight.

"They'll eat us alive," she gasped. "We've got to get out of here, and fast."

There was a sudden loud crash from outside, and then screams. Smoke billowed in under the barn door.

"The Beast!" came a shout from nearby. "It's here!"

"If there is a Beast out there, it's not Hawkite," muttered Elenna.

As if to confirm their fears, the ground shook, as though with the footsteps of something huge.

Whatever's out there, thought Tom, *it's something massive...*

THE PRIZE RAM

Tom's eyes stung with the smoke pouring into the barn. The rats scurried away into the shadows, as a lick of flame shot up from under the wooden door. Then another.

Pretty soon the whole building will be ablaze!

Tom squirmed, trying to kick his way free. He felt the cartwheel shift beneath him as he struggled, but the ropes still held him in place.

"Wait – I've got an idea!" called Elenna. She began moving again, but instead of fighting against the ropes, she threw her weight to one side. There was a rumbling sound as her cartwheel turned, edging closer to Tom.

"Of course!" said Tom. He copied her, leaning to one side with all his weight until his own wheel creaked into motion. Slowly, the cartwheel turned until Tom was upside down, with the blood pounding in his ears. He could feel the wheel wobbling, and he tensed every muscle in his body to stop it from falling on its side.

We just need to keep up the momentum...

Sweat broke out on Tom's brow as he turned the wheel again. It was all he could do to keep it moving. He twisted his neck, and through the thickening smoke he could just make out the barn wall, already crackling with flames.

Tom felt his heart lurch. If they weren't going fast enough to smash right through the wall, they would be trapped in the fire with no hope of escape. They'd be burned to death...

He threw all his weight into the cartwheel, and gradually, it began

to speed up. The world blurred,
turning round and round and
making Tom's head spin until he
didn't know which way was up.

Smoke filled his eyes, his mouth
and his nostrils, blinding him,
choking him.

Any second now...

Smash!

Splinters exploded all around
him, and the air was suddenly cool
on his face. The wheel tottered
and fell with Tom facing upwards,
juddering his bones as it hit the
ground. The next moment Elenna's
came crashing down next to it.

Tom stared dizzily up at the
stars, which seemed to be dancing

like crazy. His stomach turned
somersaults. But none of that
mattered.

We made it!

A long-haired figure appeared in his vision, blocking out the night sky.

"That was amazing!" said Kevan. He knelt over Tom, a sword in his hand. *My sword*, Tom realised. He saw that the boy was wearing his belt and scabbard too, though it scraped the ground. On his back he'd slung Elenna's bow and quiver.

Kevan sawed at the ropes until Tom was able to stagger upright, rubbing at the marks around his wrists. Then the boy turned to Elenna, cutting her free too.

"You're a hero, Kevan," Elenna told him, as she took her weapons back.

The little boy blushed deeply. "There's a Beast on the rampage," he said, breathlessly. "I'm going to help you fight it!"

The ground trembled, and a thunderous rumble echoed all around.

Tom turned and saw they were on a muddy patch of village green, surrounded by rough wooden sheds and houses and lit by the burning of several buildings.

The ground shook again, and a huge wooden cowshed nearby shuddered, as though it might fall to pieces at any moment. From behind the building came a gust of foul green smoke, and a snuffling, snorting noise.

The Beast!

Kevan had turned as white as a ghost.

"Get out of here while you can," Tom told him.

The boy hesitated, then shook his head. "I'm not going anywhere. My people wanted the rats to eat you! The least I can do is help you protect our home."

Tom felt his lips twitch into a grim smile. "Very well then," he said. "We'll face it together."

Slowly but surely, the Beast came into view. First his head emerged from behind the building, snorting green smoke. Tom felt a little shiver run down his spine at the sight. The Beast had huge curling horns and sickly orange eyes that crawled from side to side, hunting for prey.

His body came next, massively
muscled and covered in a shaggy
mane of hair. His hooves sank deep
into the ground, each one dripping
a foul-smelling green goo that

sizzled wherever it fell.

Kevan let out a gasp. "But that's...
It's Ronak!"

"Who's Ronak?" asked Elenna.

"It's Karl's prize ram!" said

Kevan. "But something terrible must have happened to him. He's turned into a monster!"

Tom nodded. "That's how Kensa creates her Beasts. By using evil magic on innocent creatures."

"So it really was Kensa who put those bits of fleece outside Hawkite's cave," said Elenna. "She'll pay for this."

Tom turned back to the Beast, and froze. Ronak was staring right at them, his eyes glowing like hot coals. And before they could react, the monstrous ram lowered his head, lifted a nearby cart with his horns and tossed it up into the air.

The cart crashed down onto

the village green, exploding into
splinters.

Elenna drew an arrow and loosed
it, sending it whirring at the Beast.

The missile glanced off one of the Beast's horns and smacked into the wall of the cowshed. Elenna was already fitting another to her bowstring.

Kevan stood still as a statue. Tom lifted his sword gently from the boy's trembling hand, then took Kevan by the arm and hustled him across the green to the wreckage of the cart.

"Hide under here," he told the boy, speaking as calmly as he could. "Don't come out, whatever happens. We'll deal with Ronak."

The boy managed to nod before crawling under the broken cart.

Tom drew himself up, feeling the weight of the sword in his hand.

He turned and saw Elenna's third arrow slam into the Beast's fleece. But Ronak didn't seem to notice it. He stamped the ground with a front hoof, and let out a rumbling roar that made Tom's stomach squirm.

"He's going to charge!" Elenna shouted.

Sure enough, the Beast surged forward. The thundering of his hooves made the ground shudder so that Tom could barely stay on his feet.

My sword will be useless against him, Tom realised. *He's going too fast...*

As the Beast loomed closer, Tom hurled himself to one side, rolling

in the mud as Ronak stampeded past. The monstrous ram carried on without even a backward glance.

Wait – so he wasn't heading for me after all!

Tom leapt to his feet, drawing on the power of the golden leg armour. The magic surged into his legs, giving him a burst of incredible speed as he took off in pursuit of the ram.

Ahead, Ronak was charging full tilt into a house at the end of the street. He lowered his head and slammed into the side.

The impact made the wall cave in, sending a cloud of dust into the air as the thatched roof collapsed inwards. Tom heard screams from inside the house as Ronak backed off, shaking broken bits of timber from its horns. The Beast let out an angry roar.

Tom skidded to a halt. The dust was clearing, and he saw a family huddled in the ruins of their house. Two small girls clung to their mother's apron, while their father held his arms protectively around them. A young man, with wild dark hair...

Karl.

"Ronak?" Karl pleaded. Tom could hear the tremble of terror in his voice. "It's me! I've taken good care of you since you were a little lamb... You must recognise us!"

Ronak let out another ear-splitting bellow and reared up on his hind legs, hooves dripping toxic poison, casting a shadow over the defenceless family.

Tom's blood froze.

He's going to crush them to death!

6

POISON!

The ground was scattered with broken bits of wood from Ronak's rampage, and Tom snatched up the heaviest he could lift. He took aim and sent it hurtling at the Beast, drawing on the power of the golden breastplate to throw it as hard as he could.

The chunk of timber smacked into

the ram's back, knocking him
off course as his hooves came
plunging down.

Thump!

Ronak's forelegs fell heavily into the street beside the house, as Karl led his family clambering out of the rubble on the opposite side. The Beast let out another bellow of rage and turned, stamping the dirt with his hooves as his mad orange eyes searched for whoever had thrown the missile...

Elenna came racing to Tom's side. "Good work, Tom," she said breathlessly. "But we have to get that Beast out of the village. And quickly, before he tramples the whole place to dust."

"I'll take you to the horses!" called a familiar voice. Tom turned and saw that Kevan had followed them.

His face was smeared with soot, but he looked as determined as ever. "They're in the stables over there," he said, pointing.

"Kevan, you really have to hide this time," Elenna said sternly, as Tom set off running towards the building the boy had indicated.

No chance of that, Tom thought. *Kevan's got more guts than anyone else in this village!*

The stable doors were hanging open, and Tom dived inside. Angel and Star whinnied at the sight of him, and he untied them fast, vaulting up onto Angel's back as Elenna followed and climbed onto Star.

Just as Tom kicked his horse's flank, he felt someone leap up behind him. *Kevan!* But before he could make the boy dismount, there was a thunderous sound from above, and the roof exploded in a shower of broken timber. A hoof came pounding down, narrowly missing them as it slammed into the floor.

"Let's get out of here!" yelled Elenna.

Tom didn't need telling twice. He flicked the reins and dug in his heels. Angel shot out of the gates, and Tom felt the wind full in his face as they raced through the village.

"Hang onto my waist," Tom

called over his shoulder, and he felt
Kevan's arms flung around him,
clinging on so tight it was almost
painful.

"Elenna," Tom shouted. "Can you
get that Beast's attention?"

His friend nodded, as she galloped
alongside on Star. The next moment
Elenna had nocked an arrow and
sent it zipping back at Ronak. Tom
turned and saw the missile strike
the ram squarely in the chest. The
Beast reared up and charged after
them, smashing aside tools, barrels
and fences as he careered down the
street.

"I hope you've got a good plan!"
yelled Elenna, as she took up the

reins and sped alongside.

I hope so too, thought Tom.

They swerved around a corner and saw open fields ahead. Angel was panting now and lathered in sweat. Tom willed the horse to keep going.

But he could feel his steed flagging as they leapt over a low wall and raced on into the night.

"Tom, the horses..." shouted Elenna.

"I know!" Tom called back. "They can't take much more."

We'll have to face the Beast soon. But how? They'd already tried Tom's sword and Elenna's arrows, and the weapons were useless against Ronak.

Behind them the giant ram was gaining, shaking the ground with his hooves, filling Tom's ears with his angry snorting.

The sounds brought back a memory. Back in Errinel, where

Tom was raised, one of the farmers had owned a ram just like Ronak – or just like Ronak must have been before Kensa got her hands on him! Tom had once helped the farmer and his son move the ram between fields, when he was half asleep.

Wait – half asleep...

"Tom?" called Kevan. "What are we going to do?"

But Tom ignored him. Gradually the memory was returning. The farmer had fed the ram some special seeds crushed into his mash. "They'll make the old boy drowsy," he'd told Tom. "Then he'll be easier to shift – you'll see."

It hit Tom like a lightning bolt. *We*

might not be beaten yet!

Angel leapt over a narrow stream. As they landed, Kevan's hands slipped from Tom's waist.

"No!" screamed the boy. But it was too late – he was already tumbling towards the ground.

Tom's heart lurched. "Keep going," he shouted at Elenna. Then he unhooked the bag tied to Angel's harness with one hand and swung his leg over the horse, diving for the ground and landing in a roll. The thump of the impact took the wind out of him, but he staggered to his feet and rushed over to Kevan, who was sprawled face down on the muddy bank of the stream.

Tom bent over the boy, his blood
turning ice-cold in his veins. Kevan
had fallen into a thick green puddle
of the Beast's poison, and his
face was totally submerged. Tom
rolled him onto his back, wiping
the boy's face with a sleeve, but

even underneath the foul-smelling sludge, Kevan's skin was tinged with green, and his eyes were closed.

"Is he all right?" Elenna called. Tom looked up to see that she had pulled up Star and caught Angel by the reins.

"He's been poisoned," Tom replied. He heaved Kevan up and over his shoulder, casting a glance back at Ronak. The Beast was still coming for them, an unstoppable juggernaut getting closer by the second. Quickly Tom carried the boy to Elenna and threw him over the back of the horse.

"Get Kevan to safety," said Tom. "He'll need your healing

herbs if he's to survive."

"What about you?" asked Elenna.

"Don't worry about me," Tom told her. "I'll hold Ronak off for as long as I can."

Elenna hesitated, and for a moment Tom thought she was going to argue with him. Then she nodded. "Good luck," she said, before kicking her heels and riding off into the darkness, with Kevan at her back, and Angel at her side.

Tom took a deep breath.

I'm all on my own now.

Then he turned to face Ronak.

STOMPED TO DEATH

The Beast skidded to a halt on the other side of the stream. Moonlight glinted off the ridged curves of his horns, and his orange eyes glowed with malice.

It's Kensa's magic, Tom had to remind himself, as he unslung his shield. *Ronak isn't really evil.*

Suddenly the giant ram tensed his back legs and launched himself across the stream, his hooves plunging towards Tom like two great anvils. Tom hurled himself to one side as the hooves hit the bank, spattering him with mud.

Before Tom could get to his feet the Beast was slamming his hooves down a second time, so close Tom felt the wind as they struck the solid ground beside him with a heavy thud, oozing toxic slime.

Tom scrambled away. For a Beast that size, Ronak was fast. The ram reared up in the air, blotting out the moon with his massive bulk as he let out a rumbling bellow. Then

his hooves came down a third time,
forcing Tom to dodge yet again.

Tom was panting, his body flooded

with adrenaline.

I can't keep this up for long. If I don't fight back soon, I'll be stomped to death!

Behind his shield, his left hand held on tight to the bag he'd taken from Angel. The key to defeating Ronak was inside it...

Tom looked up to see the Beast taking small steps backwards, snorting green smoke. The next moment Ronak hurtled forward, lowering his head as he charged Tom head-on.

Tom flung up his shield desperately as the horns loomed towards him.

The blow sent a violent judder

through Tom's shield, and he
stumbled, falling in the mud. His
whole arm was numb from the
impact.

Ronak swerved and raced forward
again, his hooves kicking up

splashes of foul green goo.

This time Tom met the attack with his sword, sidestepping and slicing at Ronak's horn.

It was like striking a solid bar of iron. Tom's blade bounced off, and the full force of his blow rang through his arm, rattling his bones all over again.

Now both his arms were throbbing with pain. The Beast seemed to sense it, sniffing at the air as he swivelled and lowered his head for a third time.

You can do this, Tom told himself, as Ronak picked up speed. *You've faced hundreds of Beasts before...* But he wasn't sure he believed it.

At the last minute Tom tried to leap sideways, but his boots slipped in the mud churned up by Ronak's hooves. The Beast caught Tom's shield on his horns, lifting him up into the air and tossing him aside.

The world spun before Tom's eyes, then he hit the ground hard, pain exploding across his back. Gasping for breath, he flexed his fingers, and found that he'd dropped his sword. It was too dark to see where it had fallen.

It was useless anyway. Against this Beast, I might as well be fighting with a knitting needle!

The ground shuddered, and Tom turned to see Ronak plunging

towards him yet again. He tensed every muscle, ready to spring out of the way of the ram's deadly horns. *This is it – the killer blow.* After all his Quests, Tom was going to end his days crushed to death by nothing more terrible than a farm animal...

Ronak let out a sudden bellow, and lurched sideways, crashing down into the mud. It took Tom a moment to realise that the ram had slipped, just as he had done himself. Ronak struggled to squirm upright.

Somewhere deep inside Tom, a spark of hope flickered into life.

This is your chance.

Tom slung his shield and saddlebag on his back and leapt

forward, reaching for the Beast. Ronak was still writhing in the mud, and Tom caught hold of his curly fleece, gripping it with all his strength. The stench of the wool was noxious and overpowering, but

whatever happened, Tom knew he had to hold on.

Ronak finally staggered upright, lifting Tom with him. He snorted in confusion, peering around for his foe. Tom tried to stay utterly still, but the ram must have felt him clinging on, because suddenly he bucked savagely, almost throwing Tom clear.

Tom dug his feet into the Beast's side and pushed himself upwards, grabbing fistfuls of fleece as he went. Ronak bucked again, letting out another roar of fury as Tom swung his leg over the ram's back and hauled himself up. *Made it!* He reached inside his saddlebag,

holding his breath as he pulled out
the seaweed he had gathered on the
coast.

All at once Tom realised that the

Beast had stopped trying to throw him off. Instead the giant ram was standing utterly still, his nostrils snorting jets of foul-smelling air. Tom looked up, and his heart sank as he saw why.

A hundred paces ahead, a tree was silhouetted against the horizon, and beneath it were two horses, and two figures. Drawing on the power of the golden helmet, Tom could make them out clearly – a boy sitting with his back against the trunk, and a girl crouching over him, holding herbs to her companion's mouth.

Ronak took a step towards the tree. Then another, and another, gathering speed until Tom was jolting up and down on the Beast's back as they raced across the ground, faster than any horse.

Panic gripped Tom's whole body.

If I don't do something right now, Elenna and Kevan are going to be trampled!

8

BREATHE IN DEEP

Tom shouted at the top of his voice. "Elenna!"

His friend turned, and Tom saw her eyes go wide in shock at the sight of the Beast careering towards her. She grabbed Kevan under his arms and dragged the boy around the side of the trunk, out of the path of the Beast. Then she strode forward, fitting an arrow to her bow and dropping to one knee to aim.

Tom ducked down low on Ronak's back, as Elenna's first arrow whizzed towards them.

Whsssshhh... Thunk!

The arrow planted itself in Ronak's chest, but the Beast didn't even slow his pace. Elenna fired a second arrow, and a third.

Thunk!

Thunk!

Each one found its mark, and still Ronak showed no sign of stopping.

They were sixty paces away, then fifty, then forty...

No time to waste. Tom hauled himself forwards, using the fleece like ropes to pull himself closer to Ronak's head. Then he slid down the ram's shoulders, bracing his boots, one against each horn.

Elenna was still standing her ground. *She won't leave Kevan behind,* Tom realised. *She'd rather die than abandon him.*

Determination coursed through Tom, and he dived face forward onto Ronak's head, tensing his legs against the sides of the ram's snout and clamping the seaweed over his nose.

Ronak snorted and shook his head, but Tom held on tight.

Breathe, Ronak. Breathe in deep...

Thirty paces. Twenty-five. Twenty.

Every muscle in Tom's body burned with the effort of clinging on. But still Ronak kept going, snorting furiously. Any second now Elenna would disappear under his hooves...

Not while there's blood in my veins!

Tom pushed the seaweed right into Ronak's nostrils. The Beast threw his head violently upwards, then stumbled and let out a sound – half bellow, half groan.

Suddenly Tom's stomach flipped as he felt himself sinking with the Beast. Drawing on the power of the golden boots, he launched himself off the ram's head, aiming for Elenna. He flew through the air, landing in a roll, and spinning round to face Ronak.

The Beast came crashing towards them, his head and horns blocking out everything as he ploughed into Tom's shield.

SMASH!

Tom and Elenna were driven
backwards like leaves in the wind,
tumbling head over heels. They
bounced across the hard ground,
the shock rattling their bones. Tom
closed his eyes, waiting for it all to
be over...

When he finally came to rest he

was lying on his back, bruised and shaken. He tried to move his shield arm, but it was throbbing with pain all over again. He opened his eyes, and found that the air was filled with dust.

"Elenna!" He coughed. "Where are you?"

A creeping sense of dread stole over his skin, as he pulled himself to a sitting position. *What if she hit the tree? What if my shield didn't protect her? What if—*

"Tom!" came an answering cry. Elenna stumbled out of the dust towards him. Tom's heart leapt to see his friend alive.

"Hey," said a new voice. "What's happening?"

Tom turned to see the figure of a small boy sitting upright underneath the spreading branches of the tree, next to the horses. Kevan's face had lost its green tinge. He blinked, looking confused.

"I think I fell asleep," he

murmured. "I had such a strange dream..."

"You can tell us about it later," said Tom. "Right now we have to get away before Ronak wakes up again."

Elenna laughed. "I don't think we need to worry too much about Ronak," she said.

Tom turned. The dust had finally settled, and the Beast had disappeared. In his place a normal ram was clambering to his feet, looking just as confused as Kevan. Ronak let out a bleat. One of his horns had broken off against Tom's shield, and it lay on the ground beside his hooves. But apart from that, he looked none the worse

for Kensa's evil spell.

Tom grinned as he stepped forward, letting the creature nuzzle his hand.

"It's all right," he told it. "Everything's back to normal now."

Ronak bleated again and ambled off, unsteadily, to lap water from the stream.

"Ronak's kind of cute," said Elenna, with a wry smile. "I never would have guessed!"

The villagers had put out most of the fires by the time Tom and Elenna arrived back in Hintor. Angel and Star were glad to be trotting peacefully, and Angel didn't seem to mind the extra load of Kevan. Tom had stowed Ronak's horn safely in his bag, along with the scraps of seaweed. Elenna led Ronak with a rope halter.

Some people muttered and pointed at them as they rode through the shadowy streets, and Tom began to worry. *Do they think we're responsible for all this?* But as the village green came into view, they were met by a great cheer. Villagers were gathered in a big crowd, and at their head was Karl, beaming happily.

"You brought him back!" called Karl. He rushed forward, taking Ronak's halter from Elenna and tousling the ram's head. When he looked up at Tom and Elenna, his face was grave.

"Reckon I owe you both an apology," he said. "And Uther, and the people of Guran. They never stole Ronak, and it wasn't Hawkite, either." He shuddered. "To think what kind of foul spell was cast on my poor ram..."

"This was all Kensa's doing," Tom told him. "She's an evil sorceress, and she's trying to sow discord and hatred throughout Gwildor. I hope you'll never be unlucky enough to meet her in person."

Karl nodded. "So do I. Thank you, Master of the Beasts, for all that you've done."

Elenna reached over, giving Kevan a hand as the boy slid to the ground. Kevan was looking sheepish. "Why don't you stay a while?" he asked, twisting his hands together. "You must be tired and hungry."

Tom shook his head. "I wish we could. But I'm afraid our Quest is far from over."

He thought of the city of Jengtor – of its starving people, and of his own mother, poisoned at the hands of Kensa.

No – we can't stop now.

Kevan's face fell.

"I have a feeling we'll see you again one day soon though, Kevan," said Elenna. "You know, you're so brave, you remind me of someone." She caught Tom's eye, and gave him a wink.

At once the smile returned to

Kevan's face. "Maybe one day I'll grow up to be a great Master of the Beasts, like Tom!" he said. "Until then... Goodbye, Tom and Elenna. And good luck."

Tom smiled back at him. *Good luck...* he thought. *Where we're going, we'll need it.*

CONGRATULATIONS, YOU HAVE COMPLETED THIS QUEST!

At the end of each chapter you were awarded a special gold coin.
The QUEST in this book was worth an amazing 8 coins.

Look at the Beast Quest totem picture inside the back cover of this book to see how far you've come in your journey to become

MASTER OF THE BEASTS.

The more books you read, the more coins you will collect!

Do you want your own
Beast Quest Totem?

1. Cut out and collect the coin below
2. Go to the Beast Quest website
3. Download and print out your totem
4. Add your coin to the totem
www.beastquest.co.uk/totem

Don't miss the next exciting Beast Quest book, SOLIX THE DEADLY SWARM!

Read on for a sneak peek...

CHAPTER ONE

A STRANGER IN NEED

Tom leaned low over Angel's neck, the thud of galloping hooves jolting though his tense muscles. At his side, Elenna rode Star, her short hair tugged back by the wind.

The bright Gwildorian sky arched high above them, a cloudless blaze of sapphire blue, and rolling grassland swept by on either side. But Tom's mind's eye was turned inwards to an image of his mother, sick from an evil poison. She lay in Jengtor, the Gwildorian capital, which was under attack from the Pirate King, Sanpao. Only the Good Witch Irina's magical force field protected the citizens from Sanpao's barrage of cannon fire – and the force field was being eaten away day by day, moment by moment. Tom scanned the flat horizon, and took a deep breath, trying to control the emotions raging inside him. He and Elenna were still at least two days' ride from Jengtor. *We have to get there in time!*

Angel's hooves barely seemed to touch the ground as she flew over the grassy plains. The rushing wind cooled Tom's face, and with the release of speed, his spirits lifted. *If we keep going at this pace, we'll make up for the time we've lost defeating Kensa's enchanted Beasts.* Sanpao's witch companion had created a magical potion that could turn ordinary creatures into deadly monsters. Tom and Elenna had already battled two since their arrival in Gwildor.

Tom squinted into the sun and

noticed a dark spot streaking towards them through the sky. He called on the enhanced vision from his golden helmet, and saw at once that it was a sleek blue dove carrying a vial in its beak.

"A royal messenger from Jengtor!" he called to Elenna, tugging on the reins to bring Angel to a stop, as the bird let the tiny vial fall. Tom snatched the vial from the air.

Elenna pulled up beside him, her brows pinched together with concern. "I hope it's good news this time," she said.

Tom gritted his teeth, his chest tight with worry as he pulled the stopper from the vial. It released

billowing purple smoke, which
spread to form a swirling cloud. Then
the vapour at the centre of the cloud
thinned, forming an image of elegant

spires and graceful bridges beneath
a shimmering dome of light.

Irina's force field, Tom realised. The
Good Witch had told him she had
conjured a magical shield to protect
Jengtor from the pirates.

But the dark shape of Sanpao's
flying ship was hovering over the
dome, black cannon jutting from its
portholes. *No!* Tom's belly churned
with dread as the cannon fired a
volley of missiles towards the city.
The force field flared bright where
the cannonballs hit, and then burned
dimmer and paler once they had
tumbled away.

"Irina's magic is weakening,"
Elenna said.

Tom gripped the hilt of his sword. "I'm going to make Sanpao pay!" he said. Frustration burned in his chest as he thought of the distance they still had to travel. *I wish I had the power to step inside that vision!*

The magical image before him shifted suddenly. The viewpoint swept downwards through Irina's force field, over the broad, mansion-lined streets of Jengtor, and into the gilded palace at the heart of the city.

Tom felt his heart clench.

"Oh!" Elenna gasped. Tom's mother, Freya, lay in a four-poster bed, half hidden by richly patterned curtains. At her side, Irina leaned forward to press a damp cloth to

Freya's pale brow. Freya frowned and lifted her arm, pushing Irina's hand away. Tom felt a glimmer of hope as his mother's eyes flickered open – but there was no recognition in her misty, wide-eyed stare.

Irina stood back from the bed and turned to gaze out through the veil of purple smoke. Tom was shocked by how changed she was. Her eyes were filled with sorrow, and there were dark circles beneath them that hadn't been there before.

Read *Solix The Deadly Swarm* to find out what happens next!

Discover the new Beast Quest mobile game from

▶ PLAY GAMES

Available free on iOS and Android

  amazon.com

Guide Tom on his Quest to free the Good Beasts
of Avantia from Malvel's evil spells.

Battle the Beasts, defeat the minions,
unearth the secrets and collect
rewards as you journey through the
Kingdom of Avantia.

DOWNLOAD THE APP TO BEGIN
THE ADVENTURE NOW!